THIS WALKER BOOK BELONGS TO:

_____

_____

_____

_____

For J.W.L.
C. Mc.

First published 1981 by
Walker Books Ltd
87 Vauxhall Walk
London SE11 5HJ

This edition published 1989

Reprinted 1990
Printed in Italy by Graphicom srl

British Library Cataloguing in Publication Data
Hoban, Russell, *1925-*
The great fruit gum robbery.
I. Title   II. McNaughton, Colin
813'.54 [J]
ISBN 0-7445-1210-7

THE GREAT FRUIT GUM ROBBERY

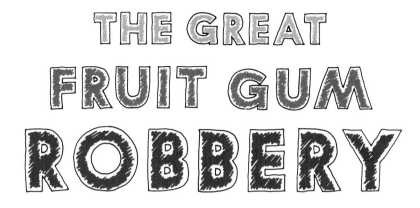

Written by

Russell Hoban

Illustrated by

Colin McNaughton

WALKER BOOKS
LONDON

There was a deep-sea diver.
He was diving, diving, swimming, swimming
far down deep. He was finding golden treasure,
secret caverns. He was swimming where the
great white shark was gliding, where the giant

clam was waiting, where the kraken groaned and slobbered. He was swimming where the crusted sunken galleons and the waving-weeded bones of dead men lay.

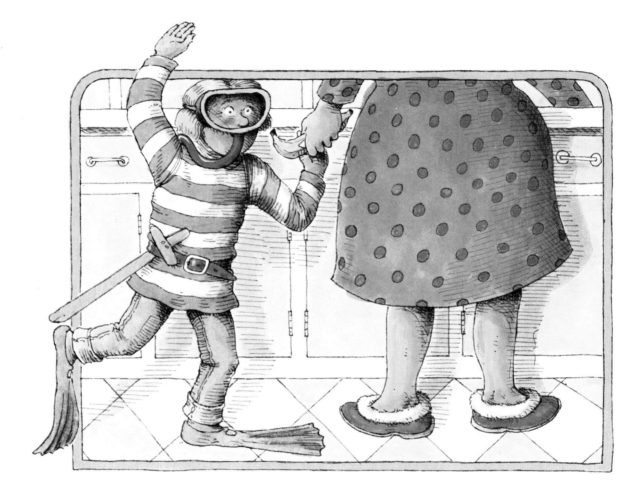

When he was hungry he told the mermaid queen.
She gave him food.

When he needed rubber bands or sticky tape
he got them from the mermaid king.

Sometimes he visited the king of the desert. The king of the desert had oases and camels, he had dates and fruit gums, he had a wondrous steed named Kyrat, he had a stethoscope and a first-aid kit.

The king of the desert said to the deep-sea
diver, "Do you have any great white shark bites?"
The deep-sea diver said, "Here and here.
Can I have a fruit gum?"

The king of the desert said, "No, I'll give you two sticking plasters."

The deep-sea diver said, "Thank you very much but I'd like a fruit gum as well please."

The king of the desert said, "I haven't got any fruit gums."

The deep-sea diver said, "What are those right there in your oasis then?"
The king of the desert said, "Those are guit frums. Better let me listen to your heart."
The deep-sea diver said, "If you want to listen to my heart you have to give me a guit frum."

The king of the desert quickly picked up his oasis. He said, "Never mind then, I am going to mount Kyrat swift and fleet and gallop far away."

Just then there roared up on a motorcycle
the baby Turpin.
"Quick!" said the deep-sea diver to the baby
Turpin. "After him!"

The king of the desert was galloping far away
but the baby Turpin was after him.
"Faster!" shouted the king of the desert to Kyrat.

Behind him blew the dust and sand cloud
of his riding.
The baby Turpin's motorcycle roared.

From his motorcycle leapt the baby Turpin
on to Kyrat's croup. The baby Turpin
grabbed the king of the desert's oasis and

he ran for his life. He couldn't be bothered
with the motorcycle, he was in too much
of a hurry.

"Get him!" yelled the king of the desert.
He jumped off Kyrat and ran after the baby
Turpin. "Stop, thief!" he shouted.
"Stop, thief!" shouted the deep-sea diver.

The deep-sea diver had thought that the baby
Turpin was going to share the fruit gums with
him but the baby Turpin seemed to have
forgotten that.

The baby Turpin was out of the desert like
a shot and he was sailing away across the sea.
He went down to the bottom of the sea,

he hid in the castle of the mermaid queen
and ate up all the fruit gums while the giant
clams stood guard outside the door.

The king of the desert began to cry.
"He stole my whole oasis of fruit gums!" he said.
The deep-sea diver was crying too. "He was going
to share with me and he never did!" he said.

"Never mind," said the mermaid queen. "It's supper time anyhow."

"Yes, but what about my fruit gums?" said the king of the desert. "That really isn't fair."

The mermaid king said, "Next time you all get
sweets the baby Turpin will have to give you
some of his."
"All right," said the king of the desert. "That's fair."

The baby Turpin kissed the king of the desert.
"Oh, well," said the king of the desert, "I don't
mind if he has a few extra fruit gums, really.
He needn't give me any next time."

The baby Turpin kissed the deep-sea diver.
"Oh, well," said the deep-sea diver, "he gave me
some of his fruit gums last time. He isn't
so bad, really."

Then they all had supper.

MORE WALKER PAPERBACKS

THE PRE-SCHOOL YEARS

John Satchwell
& Katy Sleight
Monster Maths
ODD ONE OUT   BIG AND LITTLE
COUNTING   SHAPES   ADD ONE   SORTING
WHAT TIME IS IT?   TAKE AWAY ONE

FOR THE VERY YOUNG

John Burningham
Concept books
COLOURS   ALPHABET
OPPOSITES   NUMBERS

Byron Barton
TRAINS   TRUCKS   BOATS   AEROPLANES

PICTURE BOOKS
For All Ages

Colin McNaughton
THERE'S AN AWFUL LOT OF WEIRDOS IN
OUR NEIGHBOURHOOD
SANTA CLAUS IS SUPERMAN

Russell Hoban
& Colin McNaughton
The Hungry Three
THEY CAME FROM AARGH!
THE GREAT FRUIT GUM ROBBERY

Jill Murphy
FIVE MINUTES' PEACE
ALL IN ONE PIECE

Bob Graham
THE RED WOOLLEN BLANKET
HAS ANYONE HERE SEEN WILLIAM?

Philippa Pearce
& John Lawrence
EMILY'S OWN ELEPHANT

David Lloyd
& Charlotte Voake
THE RIDICULOUS STORY OF
GAMMER GURTON'S NEEDLE

Nicola Bayley
Copycats
SPIDER CAT   PARROT CAT   CRAB CAT
POLAR BEAR CAT   ELEPHANT CAT

Peter Dallas-Smith
& Peter Cross
TROUBLE FOR TRUMPETS

Philippe Dupasquier
THE GREAT ESCAPE

Sally Scott
THE THREE WONDERFUL BEGGARS

Bamber Gascoigne
& Joseph Wright
AMAZING FACTS BOOKS 1 & 2

Martin Handford
WHERE'S WALLY?
WHERE'S WALLY NOW?